RAINY SUNDAY

ELEANOR SCHICK

THE DIAL PRESS · NEW YORK

Dial easy-to-read

Published by
The Dial Press
1 Dag Hammarskjold Plaza
New York, New York 10017

Library of Congress Cataloging in Publication Data
Schick, Eleanor, 1942– Rainy Sunday.
Summary: A young girl enjoys some unexpected
pleasures on a rainy day.
[1. Family life—Fiction.
2. Rain and rainfall—Fiction] I. Title.
PZ7.S3445Rai [E] 80-11596
ISBN 0-8037-7371-4 (pbk.)
ISBN 0-8037-7369-2 (lib. bdg.)

The art for each picture consists of a pencil drawing
and three halftone separations.

Reading Level 2.3

For Laura and David

CONTENTS

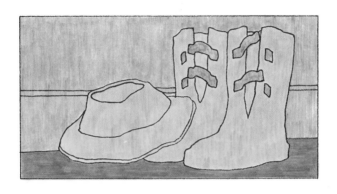

1

LOOKING OUT
MY WINDOW

It is Sunday,

but the sun did not come out.

I look out my window and see

that everything is gray.

The sky is gray.

The trees are gray.

The houses and the streets are gray.

At the corner a red light
is flashing on and off
through the gray mist.

There is a lady

carrying a gray umbrella.

She is wearing a gray raincoat.

An old man with a cane

is walking a gray dog.

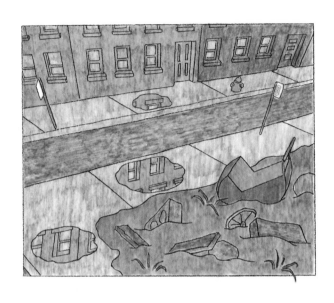

In the empty lot

where the house burned down

last year,

there are gray stones

and burned black wood.

Between the stones and wood
grass is growing.
In the grass
I can see one red flower.

2

IN MY ROOM

The walls of my room look gray
without the sun shining in.
The dial on my clock glows
because it is so dark.

My mother and father

are sleeping late.

That is why the house is so quiet.

It seems cold.

I think it will rain.

I will not be able to play outside.

I put on pants and a sweater.

I put on my warm slippers.

I am warm, but I feel sad
because the day is so dark.

I turn on my yellow lamp.
It looks like the sun
shining on my dolls.

I like my bright sweater and pants.

I find my orange ribbon.

I will wear it in my hair!

3

BREAKFAST

I hear my mother in the kitchen,
cooking breakfast.
When I come in, she asks,
"Do you want some hot oatmeal?"

I love oatmeal,

but today it looks so gray.

I put some yellow butter on

and watch it melt.

I pour a pool of yellow honey on top

and a river of white milk

around the sides.

I make lines with my spoon

from the yellow in the middle

to the white around the sides.

They look like the rays of the sun.

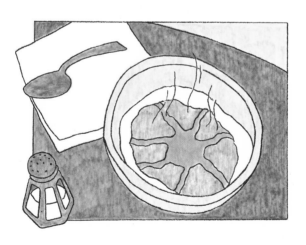

Each bite is warm and sweet.

Then Mother brings in
a tin of fresh-baked muffins.
We both have hot muffins
with peach jam.

4

SUNDAY PAPERS

My father is in the living room,
reading the Sunday papers.
The pages are black and white.
Outside, the rain is pouring down.

I take my book

and curl up on the couch

near my father.

Inside the pile of newspapers

on the table

is a page

of bright-colored comics.

I reach in and take them out.

My father puts down
his part of the paper.
We read the comics together.
I read to him,
and then he reads to me.

31

My mother comes in with her sewing.

She listens while I read.

"Jill, you're becoming

a very good reader," she says.

5

MY MOTHER'S
SEWING BASKET

Mother is making

a hem on my new skirt.

I stand on a chair

so she can pin it up.

I see a piece of bright yellow cloth

in my mother's sewing basket.

She says that I may have it.

I can use it as a rug

when I give my dolls lunch.

My dolls like the new rug,

and they like the lunch

I am making for them.

The red buttons are apples,

and the orange ones

are sweet potatoes.

The thimble is the cup

that they are sharing for milk.

6

GOING FOR A WALK

When it stops raining,
it is still cold and gray.
I finish my homework
and wonder what to do.

My mother says,

"I'm going out to mail a letter.

Would you like

to come with me?"

"Yes!" I say.

Mother tells me

to wear my raincoat and boots

in case it rains again.

The hallway is dark and still.
Our boots make an echo
as we walk down the stairs.

Outside,

the sky is silver-gray.

The puddles are like mirrors

of the houses and the sky.

45

We walk past the empty lot
where the house burned down
last year.

My mother mails her letter.
I see the red flower.

I pick the flower

while my mother waits.

When we get home,

I fill a glass with water.

I put my red flower in it.

7

RAINY DAY SUPPER

The sky is dark.

I have an early bath.

I put on my pajamas

and my robe.

I can smell the soup

that has been cooking

all afternoon.

I set the table with the red cups

we sometimes use at breakfast.

I find some orange napkins.

They were left over from Halloween.

I put my red flower

on the yellow cloth Mother gave me.

It all looks bright and cheerful.

My father makes popcorn.
He brings it to the table
in a basket.

We all sit down

to our rainy day Sunday supper.

Just before I get in bed,

I turn on the radio.

The weatherman says

tomorrow will be

a warm, sunny day.